ORLAND PARK PUBLIC LIBRARY
3 1315 00386 6261

P9-EFI-243

The Big Day at School

by Eleanor Fremont
illustrated by Michael Lennicx

Simon Spotlight/Nick Jr.
New York London Toronto Sydney Singapore

Based on the TV series *Little Bill*® created by Bill Cosby as seen on Nick Jr.®

SIMON SPOTLIGHT
An imprint of Simon & Schuster Children's Publishing Division
1230 Avenue of the Americas, New York, New York 10020

Manufactured in the United States of America
First Edition 10 9 8 7 6 5 4 3 2 1
ISBN 0-689-85497-8

One Tuesday afternoon Little Bill's mom, Brenda, picked him up at school.
"You look a little upset, Little Bill," said Brenda. "Is everything all right?"
"I don't want to go to school tomorrow," said Little Bill.

"How come?" asked Brenda. "You usually love school."

"Miss Murray told us today that she has to go to a wedding," said Little Bill. "It's far away. She'll be gone for three whole days!"

"I see," his mother said. "What will your class do while she's away?"

"She said we're going to have a substitute teacher. What if the substitute isn't nice?"

"You know," said Brenda, "I remember another time you were nervous about school."

"When?" asked Little Bill.

"Do you remember how scared you felt before you started kindergarten?"

Little Bill tried to remember his first day of kindergarten.

On the morning of Little Bill's first day of kindergarten he had more worries than he could count. He was worried that he wouldn't know any of the kids. He was afraid that his new teacher would be very strict. What if he had to act all grown-up every minute and not even sing any songs?

"Don't worry, Little Bill," Brenda said as she walked him inside the school. "Fuchsia's going to be there, and I heard your teacher's very nice."

When Little Bill got to his classroom, a friendly woman wearing glasses came over to him. Little Bill held on to his mom's hand.

"Hi, Little Bill!" she said. "I'm Miss Murray. Welcome to kindergarten!"

"Wow!" Little Bill whispered to his mother. "My teacher already knows my name!"

Little Bill let go of his mother's hand. "I'm going to play with Fuchsia," he said.

Brenda smiled and hugged him. "I'll pick you up right here at the end of the day, okay?"

Little Bill hugged her back. "Okay. Bye, Mom!"

On his way over to play with Fuchsia, Little Bill saw Andrew, his friend from the neighborhood.

"Hi, Andrew, I didn't know you were in my class!" said Little Bill excitedly.

"Me neither!" said Andrew.

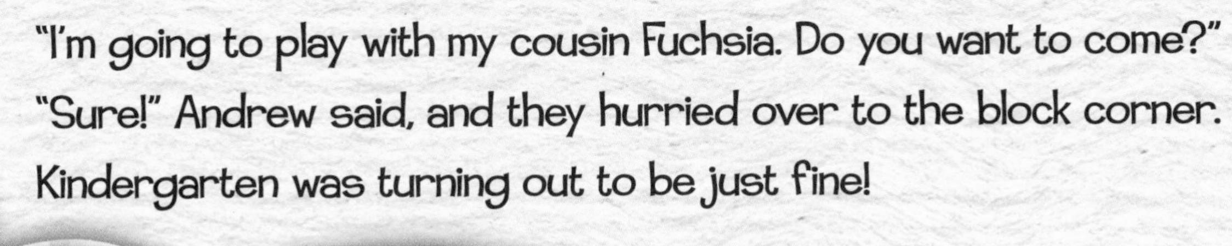

"I'm going to play with my cousin Fuchsia. Do you want to come?"

"Sure!" Andrew said, and they hurried over to the block corner.

Kindergarten was turning out to be just fine!

After the parents left, Miss Murray clapped her hands. "Okay, everybody. We're going to start the day with Circle Time," she said. "When we go around the circle, say your name and what you want to be when you grow up."

Little Bill sat next to Fuchsia. A girl sitting across from him went first.

"I'm Kiku, and I want to be president of the United States," she said.

Wow, thought Little Bill, I don't know anyone who wants to be president! Little Bill was a little nervous when it was his turn, but he saw Kiku smiling at him, so he felt better.

"I'm Little Bill and I want to be an astronaut!" he said.

After lunch Miss Murray sat down with Little Bill while he was coloring. He told her a story he made up about the Space Explorers, and she wrote it down. Then he drew pictures to go with the story.

"You know what? We can staple the pages together and make a real book," said Miss Murray.

When they finished making the book, the cover read "By Little Bill."

"I can't wait to show my mom!" he said.

Later in the afternoon Little Bill learned how to feed Wabbit, the class rabbit. He was even allowed to hold Wabbit in his hands—*very* carefully.

Then Miss Murray let them choose picture books to look at. After a little while Miss Murray said it was almost time to go home.

"But I'm not finished with my book," said Little Bill.

"You can take it home and bring it back tomorrow," said Miss Murray.

"Thanks!" said Little Bill as he put the book in his backpack.

"Tomorrow," said Miss Murray before they left, "we're going to learn a new song!"

"I like kindergarten a lot," Little Bill whispered to Kiku.

"Me too. I'm excited for tomorrow!" she said.

Little Bill laughed as he finished remembering his first day of kindergarten.

"See, Little Bill," said Brenda, "you were nervous at first, but how do you feel about school now?"

"I love school!" said Little Bill. "So I was scared for nothing."

"Well, sometimes new things are scary before you get to know them," said his mother.

"Like a substitute teacher?" asked Little Bill.

"Could be," said his mother with a smile.

The next day at school Little Bill met the substitute teacher, Mr. Franklin, who was very tall and very funny. He wore a purple bow tie and told lots of great stories.

"I was a little nervous, but Mr. Franklin is really nice," Kiku said.

"Sometimes new things are scary until you get to know them," said Little Bill, and he smiled a big smile.